THE BIG ROCK

Also written and illustrated by Bruce Hiscock
Tundra: The Arctic Land

THE BIG ROCK

written and illustrated by
BRUCE HISCOCK

ALADDIN PAPERBACKS

Thanks to William L. Murphy-Rohrer, B.S., M.R.P., Ph.D.,
Senior Geologist and Vice President,
Pope-Reid Associates, St. Paul, Minnesota,
for his expert advice.

First Aladdin Paperbacks edition December 1999

Aladdin Paperbacks
An imprint of Simon & Schuster Children's Publishing Division
1230 Avenue of the Americas
New York, NY 10020

Also available in an Atheneum Books for Young Readers hardcover edition.
Typeset by V&M Graphics, New York City
Designed by Bruce Hiscock
Typography by Mary Ahern

Printed and bound in China
10 9 8 7 6 5 4 3

The Library of Congress has cataloged the hardcover edition as follows:
Hiscock, Bruce.
The big rock / written and illustrated by Bruce Hiscock.
—1st ed.
p.   cm.
Summary: Traces the origins of a granite rock located near the Adirondack
Mountains and describes how it reveals information about the history
of the earth.
ISBN 0-689-31402-7 (hc.)
1. Rocks—Juvenile literature. 2. Geology—Juvenile literature.
I. Title.
[DNLM: 1. Rocks. 2. Geology.]
QE432.2.H57   1988
552—dc19   87-31834
CIP   AC
ISBN 0-689-82958-2 (pbk.)

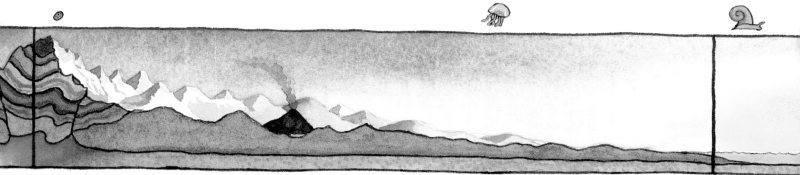

1000 million years ago

*Granite layer formed
under ancient mountains*

Mountains wear down

570

To Sue

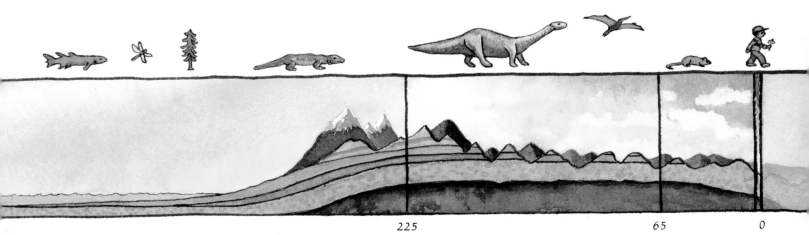

Seas and sediment
cover granite

225
Adirondack Mountains rise and wear down

65

0
Ice age
Glacier creates the big rock

One day in early spring, the last bit of snow melted from the top of the big rock. The water ran slowly across the rough surface, and then trickled down the cracks in the rock's steep sides.

It had been a hard winter. The trees nearby had lost many limbs in the heavy snow, but the big rock was almost unchanged. It was much, much older than the forest, and one more winter had little effect on it.

The big rock sits on a hillside at the southern edge of the Adirondack Mountains in New York State. This is good country for rocks. The soil in the broad valley below the hill is full of rounded stones, and rocks are scattered everywhere in the mountains to the north.

There are many places, in the northern part of the world, where the land is stony and dotted with rounded boulders. Geologists, the scientists who study the earth, wondered why this region was so rocky. They discovered that huge sheets of ice, called glaciers, had covered these northern areas just a few thousand years ago. The glaciers acted like bulldozers and spread rocks, including the big rock, all across the land.

The full story of the big rock begins long before the glaciers, however, for this is an ancient piece of stone.

All rocks, big or small, were once part of the earth's crust. The crust is a shell of solid rock, many miles thick, that covers the entire planet. Beneath the crust, the rock is so hot it is like melted plastic.

The earth's crust is made of layers of different kinds of stone. Some layers are almost as old as the earth itself, while at the bottom of the ocean volcanic lava is adding new layers right now.

The top of the crust, called bedrock, is usually hidden under soil or water, but it can be seen in stone outcrops, canyons, and cliffs.

The big rock is a chunk of granite that comes from a very old part of the earth's crust. The granite was formed about a billion years ago, under a tall mountain range in what is now New York State. The tremendous forces that pushed and folded the crust into mountains also heated the rock deep in the crust, causing some of it to melt. When the liquid rock cooled, it became granite, a hard stone full of small crystals.

At that time there were almost no living things on earth except algae, similar to green pond scum.

As the ages passed, the mountains above the granite were worn down by the weather until the hidden rock lay bare. Then the ocean crept in, flooding the region with shallow seas.

Simple plants and primitive animals, like trilobites and snails, lived in the warm waters.

TRILOBITE

The seas lasted millions of years, depositing
layers of finely ground silt and sand, called sediment,
on the granite. In time this sediment hardened into
new layers of rock. Beach sand became sandstone.
The layers of snail and trilobite shells, which contain
lime, turned into limestone. A few unbroken shells
became fossils.

The seas remained until new mountains began to rise. The granite was slowly heaved upward, carrying the sandstone and limestone along. Earthquakes now shook the land as the rock was raised and stretched to form the peaks and valleys of the Adirondack Mountains.

At first the mountains were tall and jagged.
But gradually rain, snow, wind, and frost wore away
at them. This process, called erosion, removed
the layers of sandstone and limestone from the
high places.

During this time dinosaurs appeared on the
earth. For millions of years they roamed the lowlands
while the mountains were wearing down.

The age of dinosaurs ended, but the erosion
went on and on. Finally the granite of the big rock
was exposed, perhaps as a craggy mountain peak.

The erosion of the mountains continued at a slow pace until a curious change took place in the earth's climate. A long period of cooler weather set in. The winter snow that fell near the Arctic did not melt in the summer.

Each year brought a new layer of snow. As the snowfields became larger and deeper, the bottom layers turned to ice. A glacier was forming.

The glacier grew, and its immense weight caused the ice to flow, like pancake batter, over the land. The ice age had begun.

The glaciers of the ice age were enormous,
miles thick in places. The ice covered most of
Canada and spread into the northern United States.
Glaciers formed in Europe and Asia too.

As the ice moved south, it scoured the land,
plowing up forests and bedrock.

When the glacier reached the Adirondack
Mountains, it tore at the summits and dug into the
valleys. The big rock was ripped from the granite
peak and swept away by the ice.

The glacier carried tons of rock as it flowed south. Stones beneath the ice were tumbled on the bedrock until they were round and smooth. Many rocks were crushed into gravel and sand.

The glacier continued to spread until the climate changed again. Warmer weather returned about eleven thousand years ago, and the ice began to melt.

As the glacier melted, it released the stones and gravel it carried. The big rock was dropped on the hillside miles away from where it began. The hillside was a stony, barren place then.

As the ice left the land, the wind brought seeds
and spores of plants. Moss took hold between the
stones. Later, ferns and grass sprouted. The plants
grew, and their dead stems and leaves mixed with
the sand and silt to form a thin layer of soil.

Animals returned too. Caribou and mastodon
moved north to feed in the new meadows and swamps.
The first people came to the valley about then,
following the herds of game. They were stone age
families and made spear points from pieces of rock.

Today the mastodon is extinct, and the hillside is covered with farms and forest. The big rock still looks much the same as when the glacier left, but it is slowly changing.

Each winter, water freezes in a new crack, forcing it open. This widens the crack year by year until a chip of stone breaks away. With each chip that falls, the big rock becomes a little smaller. In a few million years there may be nothing left but a lump of granite, and some sand and soil.